Once there was a boy named Tim
whom no one believed.

When his mum asked him where the last slice of cake was,
he told her the truth.

'It was a ninja!' cried Tim.

The boy who cried ninja

Alex Latimer

PICTURE CORGI

For Shann

THE BOY WHO CRIED NINJA
A PICTURE CORGI BOOK 978 0 552 56265 2
First published in Great Britain by Picture Corgi,
an imprint of Random House Children's Books
A   Random   House   Group   Company
This edition published 2011
Copyright © Alex Latimer, 2011   1 2 3 4 5 6 7 8 9 10
to be identified as the author and illustrator of this work has   The right of Alex Latimer
been asserted in accordance with the Copyright, Designs and
Patents Act 1988.   All rights reserved.   No part of this publication
may be reproduced, stored in a retrieval system, or transmitted
in any form or by any means, electronic, mechanical,
photocopying, recording or otherwise, without the prior permission
of the publishers. Picture Corgi Books are published by Random House
Children's Books, 61–63 Uxbridge Road, London W5 5SA www.rbooks.co.uk
www.kidsatrandomhouse.co.uk   Addresses for companies within The Random House
Group Limited can be found at: www.randomhouse.co.uk/offices.htm
THE RANDOM HOUSE GROUP Limited Reg. No. 954009
A CIP catalogue record for this book is
available   from   the   British   Library
Printed in China

A ninja crept into the house . . .

kicked the cake into the air
and ate it in one go.

When his dad asked him where the hammer was,
he told him the truth.

An astronaut landed in the garden and needed it
to fix his spaceship . . .

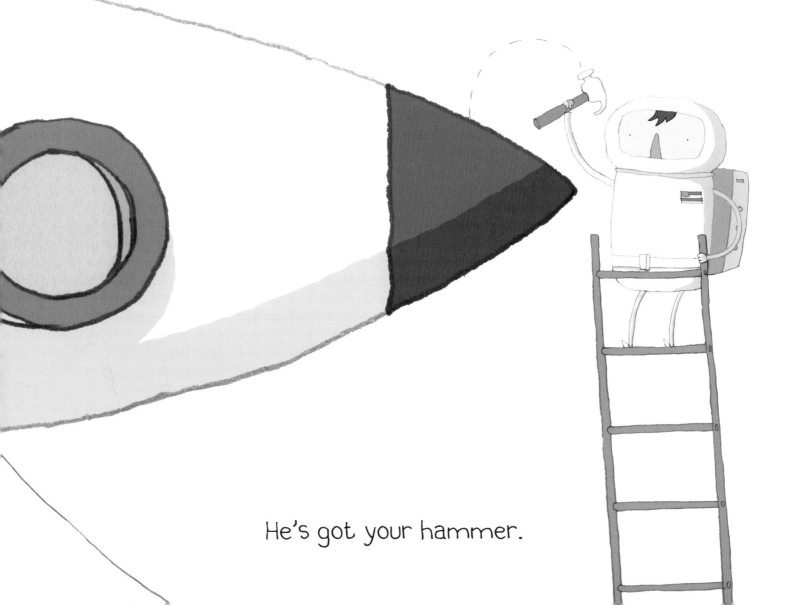

He's got your hammer.

And when Grampa asked him if he'd done his homework,
he told him the truth.

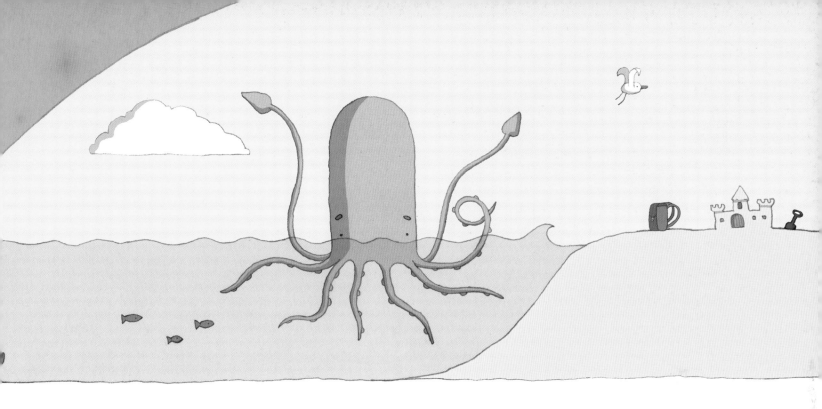

A giant squid ate my whole school bag
while I was off buying an ice cream.

But the more he thought about it,
the more he thought that perhaps he really should lie.
Then no one would be cross with him.

What else could he do?

So the next time a pirate jumped out of the cupboard . . .

and drank all the tea straight from the pot,

he owned up.

And the next time a sunburned crocodile
landed on the roof . . .

and accidentally broke
the TV aerial,

he said it was him
who'd done it.

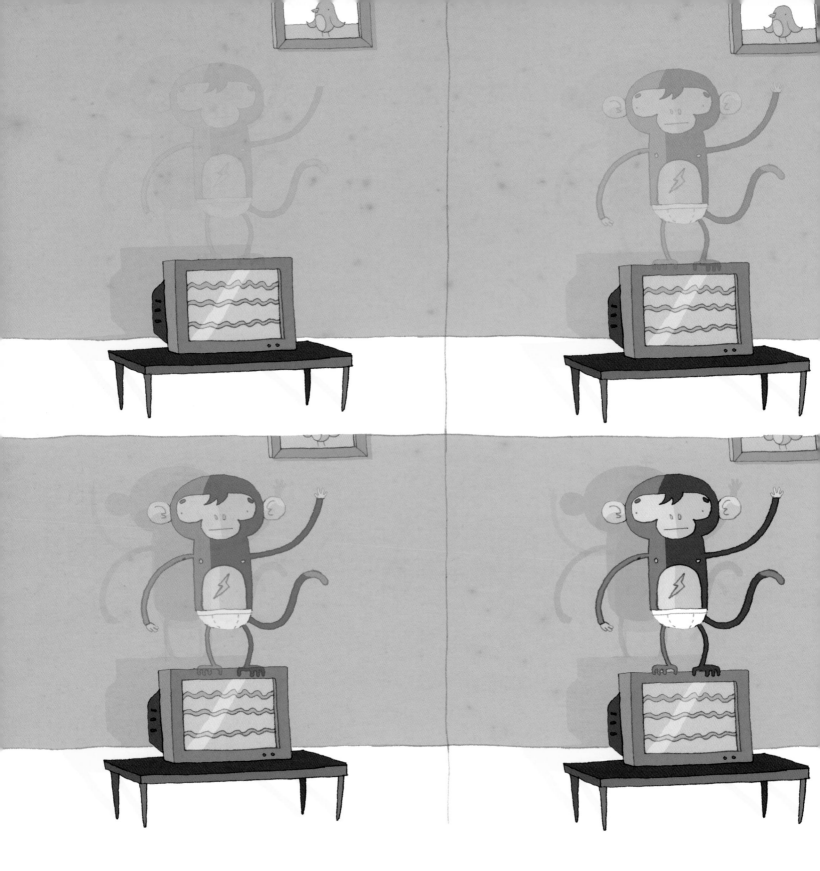

And the next time a time-travelling monkey
appeared on top of the TV . . .

and started throwing pencils at Grampa
while he was sleeping,

he said it was all his fault.

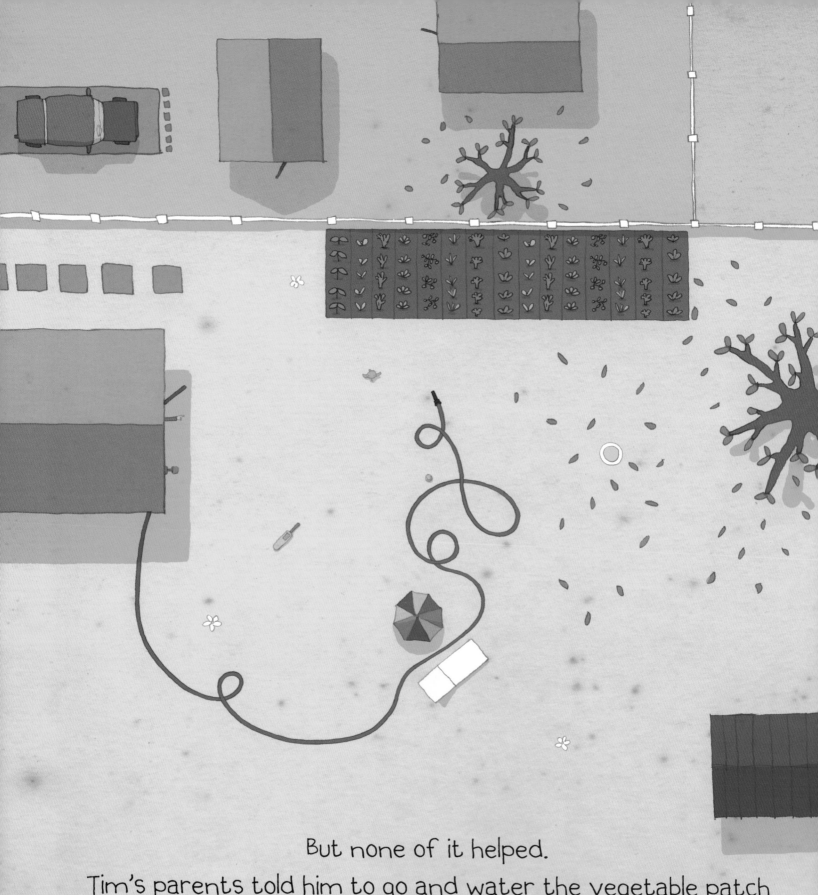

But none of it helped.
Tim's parents told him to go and water the vegetable patch
and think about all the bad things he'd done.

He found some paper
and some stamps
and he wrote six letters.

Then he went down to the post office and posted them off.

mr Squid
the ocean

Two days later six different
people received the same letter.
It went like this . . .

Dear you,
there is a party at my
house tomorrow. There
will be plenty of cake,
hammers, my new
school bag, buckets
of tea, TV aerials
and pencils.
Please come.
Me

The next day was a Saturday. Dad was fixing the house,
Grampa was reading the newspaper and Mum was vacuuming.

Then the doorbell rang. 'Who could it be?' asked Grampa.
'I'll get it,' said Tim.

There at the door stood a line of strange creatures.

First a ninja,

then an
astronaut,

a giant squid

a pirate,

a crocodile
(recently recovered
from sunburn)

and a
time-travelling
monkey.

Tim's parents could see that he'd been trying to tell the truth from the beginning. They said sorry and promised to buy him a hundred ice creams.

As for the rest of them, Tim's parents were very cross.
'Go and rake all the leaves in the garden and think about
what you've done,' said his dad.

When they had cleaned
the whole garden,
there really was a party.

And no one ate all the cake.
No one took anything without asking.
No one swallowed a school bag.
No one drank all the tea.
No one broke the aerial.
And no one threw pencils.

It was the best party Tim had ever had.

And because his parents now believed him,
he never had to cry 'ninja' ever again!

The End